Southern Love
for Christmas

By Robert Bernardini
Illustrated by James Rice

PELICAN PUBLISHING COMPANY

Gretna 1993

Library of Congress Cataloging-in-Publication Data

Bernardini, Robert.
    Southern love for Christmas / by Robert Bernardini ; illustrated
by James Rice.
        p. cm.
    Summary: Li'l Elf Jed enlists the help of his friend Annabelle
Elf to bring Christmas cheer to a gloomy Southern family.
    ISBN 0-88289-974-0
    [1. Christmas—Fiction. 2. Elves—Fiction. 3. Southern States—
Fiction. 4. Stories in rhyme.] I. Rice, James, 1934-   ill. II. Title.
PZ8.3.B458Sm   1993
[E]—dc20
                                            93-1248
                                             CIP
                                             AC

Manufactured in Hong Kong

Published by Pelican Publishing Company, Inc.
1101 Monroe Street, Gretna, Louisiana 70053

One Christmas Eve night Santa Claus was in flight
Making his holiday rounds.
With Jed in the sleigh, they sped on their way,
To farm houses, cities, and towns.

On roof tops they stopped and down chimneys they hopped,
Leaving presents with joy and good cheer,
In hopes that the feelings of peace and good will
Would continue throughout the whole year.

Then they came to a home that was standing alone,
With a chimney so tiny and small
That Santa Claus found he was too big and round
To even slide down it at all.

So Santa then said, "Jed you go instead,
And peak around quickly to find
Which gifts we should leave for this fine family,
And I'll send them right down behind!"

So Jed hopped inside that old chimney with pride,
And scampered 'round quickly to see,
A family of four sleeping on a bare floor,
Right next to a tattered old tree.

A father and mother and sister and brother,
Named Josh, Eloise, Sue, and Clem—
Their faces were drawn, and the clothes they had on
Told that hard times had come on them.

They jumped in the air when they heard Jed was there,
Surprised to see one of Nick's elves;
But Jed told them true just what he planned to do,
So they need not worry themselves.

Jed wanted to be something funny to see,
To help them forget they were down.
So on his elf head he stood till he turned red,
And acted like he was a clown.

Those folks tried to smile with Jed all the while,
And watched him with hardly a sound.
But when Jed was through, they still looked very blue,
And grumbled and looked at the ground.

The father then said, "It is hard, little Jed,
To have any holiday cheer.
It isn't too funny 'cuz we have no money
To give any presents this year."

Well, Jed's Southern wit told him never to quit
Trying to help them feel nice.
When he thought he knew, up the chimney he flew,
To whisper to Nick his advice.

"Of course!" Santa said with a nod of his head,
As Jed jumped back into the sleigh.
He pulled on the reigns, and away off they sped,
Flying south to a place far away!

In a second or three, they descended with glee
To a dwelling that sparkled and shined.
And the light from within made them chuckle and grin,
For they knew who inside they would find.

Jed sprang to the door and knocked once and twice more,
And when it swung open, there stood
An elf he knew well as his friend Annabelle,
Whose Southern charm did his heart good.

She stood there so cute in her red Christmas suit,
And her long auburn hair full of curls.
Her true Southern way made her look bright as day,
With a smile that sparkled like pearls.

"Hello Annabelle, seeing you sure is swell,"
Jed said as he held out his hand.
"Please do come with us, you're the one we can trust,
To help some poor people feel grand."

Then she did declare, "I'll be glad to go there!
But first let me gather some things.
I'll take them a treat of peach cobbler so sweet,
To go with the love Christmas brings."

So she went inside and returned full of pride,
And loaded her gifts in the sleigh.
With caring and love, she gave Santa a hug,
And soon they were off on their way.

They drank orange juice to stay limber and loose,
While flying so fast through the night.
And soon they touched down on that house with the frowns,
And squeezed down that chimney so tight.

Well, Josh and his son, sister Sue and her mom
Were still looking gloomy and glum.
So those elves dove right in with their big Southern grins,
And spread joy like a warm Southern sun.

Annabelle said, "Please be thankful instead,
And have you a good Christmas time!
Remember it isn't the presents so much
As the feeling of love that's so fine."

"Love makes you feel nice without charging a price,
'Cuz it's free and it's easy and fun!
When you choose to do it, there ain't nothin' to it,
To cheering up most anyone!"

That family of four then looked up from the floor,
And saw good in each of the others.
They all knew for sure, love is always the cure,
And the best gift to share with each other.

Those once gloomy folks now gave hugs and told jokes,
While feeling that true Southern love.
And in a short while, those two elves left in style,
Returning to Santa above.

Santa Claus said, "Annabelle and Elf Jed,
Thank you for being so true,
And sharing the meaning of Christmas with those
Who otherwise might remain blue."

"It's always more fun to laugh with your loved ones,"
He said with a wink of his eye.
With a "Ho! Ho!" and chuckle, he held his belt buckle,
And called for those reindeer to fly!

Then from that big sleigh, as they all flew away,
They sang in one voice loud and clear,
"Merry Christmas y'all! Southern love one and all!
May you have Christmas cheer all the year!"